For our children. You are never too small to make a difference. C.H.

To my parents, who taught me to love and care for nature. A.S.

First published 2022
by Nosy Crow Ltd
The Crow's Nest, 14 Baden Place
Crosby Row, London SE1 1YW
www.nosycrow.com

ISBN 978 1 78800 890 7 (HB)
ISBN 978 1 78800 891 4 (PB)

Nosy Crow and associated logos are trademarks
and/or registered trademarks of Nosy Crow Ltd

Text © Caryl Hart 2022
Illustrations © Anastasia Suvorova 2022

The right of Caryl Hart to be identified
as the author of this work and of Anastasia Suvorova
to be identified as the illustrator of this work
has been asserted.

A CIP catalogue record for this book is available
from the British Library.

Printed in China

Papers used by Nosy Crow are made from
wood grown in sustainable forests.

10 9 8 7 6 5 4 3 2 1 (HB)
10 9 8 7 6 5 4 3 2 1 (PB)

Caryl Hart

Anastasia Suvorova

# The Girl Who Planted Trees

nosy crow

Once there was a girl. She was just a small girl, about your size, actually. She lived in a dry little village at the foot of a great grey mountain.

All day long, the fierce sun scorched the earth, and when evening came, the hot air hung heavily around the houses.

One night, unable to sleep, the girl found
her grandpa reading a battered old book.

"Oh!" she gasped.
"I wish our mountain
was like that!"

"That is our mountain," sighed her grandpa.
"But year after year, the trees have been cut down
and all the animals have disappeared."

Sadly, he kissed the girl's forehead,

then tucked her back into bed.

As she ate her breakfast the next morning,
the girl thought to herself, "If only we could bring
our mountain forest back." But what could she do?
She was just one small girl . . .

Then a tiny idea caught in the corner of her mind.
"This fruit grew on a tree," she whispered.
"And here are the pips . . ."

So she gathered up some things
and set off up the mountain.

Higher and **higher** she climbed.

The rough track got steeper,
and the blistering sun scorched
the girl's back.

But she did not stop.

When, at last, she reached the top . . .

the girl began to dig into the baked earth. There she buried her pip and whispered a wish,

"Please grow, little pip."

But when she returned, eager to
see what had sprouted . . .

there was not a single
bit of green to be seen.

"Oh, Grandpa," sighed the girl. "I wanted to grow a fruit tree on the mountain, so I planted a pip. But it was a silly waste of time!"

"It was a lovely idea," said her grandpa. "But the mountain is too dry for anything much to grow. And besides, a pip can't sprout overnight! It takes days or even weeks."

"Oh!" said the girl. "In that case, I will plant some more! And this time, I will water them."

That afternoon, the girl knocked on her neighbour's door. "I'm going to grow some fruit trees on the mountain," she said. "Can you collect some pips for me?"

"Oh my!" the woman chuckled. "I've heard everything now!"

All the same, she picked out seven large pips from her peelings.

And although the girl's other
neighbours laughed too . . .

by the end of the week, she had a great number
of pips and seeds and stones of every shape and size.

"One hundred seeds will grow
one hundred trees!" the girl grinned.

Weeks passed, and each time the girl climbed the mountain, she imagined she was walking beneath a cool canopy of dappled green leaves.

How **wonderful** it would be!

Every day, she planted more seeds and watered them well.

And soon the seeds began to sprout!

Even though some withered
away under the baking sun . . .

and some were eaten by birds . . .

or dug up by animals . . .

the girl did not give up.

Until one day, some of the saplings
had grown as tall as the girl herself.
Maybe even taller than you!

"Soon I shall grow a whole
forest," she thought.

Gradually, a small patch of green began to appear on the great grey mountain. It smoothed the frowns from people's foreheads and pulled up the corners of their mouths.

Even the girl's grandpa started to feel a little lighter on his tired old legs.

Then, one sweltering night . . .

. . . a terrible storm came roaring up the valley.

Thunder boomed, lightning ripped
across the night sky, and a ferocious
wind tore through the house.

The girl huddled against her grandpa
and sobbed as if her heart might break.

"My trees!" she cried. "My poor trees!"

The storm had destroyed them all.

At home, the girl and her grandpa
slowly began to mend what was broken.

Suddenly, the girl noticed something
incredible. In the shelter of the barn,
a tiny weed stretched its petals to the sun.

"Grandpa!" she said. "The storm was too
much for my little trees, but maybe I could
grow them here until they are strong!"

In the days that followed, they filled
their yard with a higgledy-piggledy
collection of pots, jugs and pans.

And in each one,
a tiny, perfect seedling
began to grow.

But when at last her young trees were ready,
the girl became worried. "Our trees are so strong!"
she said. "But how will I carry them all the way
up the mountain?"

"You won't," said her grandpa . . .

..."We will!"

So the girl and her
grandpa filled a cart . . .

and pulled it up the mountain together.

At last, all the trees were planted, each tied to a stout stick to protect it from the blustering wind.

Still, the girl sighed.

"We have worked so hard," she said. "But it will take a thousand years to cover the whole mountain by ourselves!"

"It's lucky we are not by ourselves then," said her grandpa. "Look!"

And there below, the girl saw a great crowd of people, snaking up the mountain track towards them!

"Oh, Grandpa!" she cried.
"They're bringing the rest of our trees!"

"Yours, and many more," said
her neighbour. "You dreamed that
you could bring the forest back.
Now your dream is OUR dream too!"

Weeks turned into months,
and months stretched into years.
And just like the trees,
the girl grew tall.

She studied hard and
learned to care for the land.

All the while, everyone
worked together to look after
the trees and plant new ones.

And slowly, the great grey
mountain turned green.

Until one day, when the girl
was a grandmother herself . . .

... the mountain was even more wonderful
than the picture in her grandpa's old book.
More wonderful than anyone could ever
have imagined.

Almost as wonderful as you.